buzz buzz buzz

byron barton

aladdin paperbacks

First Aladdin Paperbacks edition 1995/Copyright © 1973 by Byron Barton/All rights reserved. Including the right of reproduction in whole or in part in any form. Aladdin Paperbacks, an imprint of Simon & Schuster Children's Publishing Division, 1230 Avenue of the Americas, New York, NY 10020. Manufactured in China.

22 23 24 25 26 27 28 29 30

1115 SCP

The text of this book is set in Olive Antique Bold.

The illustrations are rendered in pen-and-ink line drawings with overlays for yellow, red, and blue.

Library of Congress Cataloging-in-Publication Data

Barton, Byron.
    Buzz, buzz, buzz / Byron Barton. — 1st Aladdin Paperbacks ed.
        p.   cm.
    Summary: A disastrous chain of events in the farmyard begins when the bee stings the bull.
      ISBN 978-0-689-71873-1
      [1. Animals—Fiction.   2. Farm life—Fiction.   3. Humorous stories.]   I. Title.
    PZ7.B2848Bu 1995
    [E]—dc20 93-46931

buzz buzz buzz

and the bee stung the bull so hard

that the bull jumped and ran around

making the cow so nervous

that she

kicked the farmer's wife and knocked over the milk

so that the farmer's wife went home

and yelled at the farmer

making the farmer so angry

he hit the mule

who ran around behind the barn

where he kicked over the shed and

scared the goat who ran and

butted the dog into the pond

getting the dog all wet so when he saw the goose

he barked and chased her around and around until

the goose was so tired that when she saw the cat sleeping in her bed

she bit the cat's tail

and the cat jumped out the barn door

and kept on jumping after the bird who flew away

over the garden where the bird saw the bee

and dived at him

and the bee went buzz

buzz buzz

buzz buzz buzz . . .